LULLABIES

Illustrated by Hilda Offen

An index of first lines is at the back of the book

Kingfisher Books

First published in this edition in 1986
by Kingfisher Books Ltd., Elsley House,
24–30 Great Titchfield Street, London W1P 7AD
A Grisewood & Dempsey Company
Some of the material in this book is taken from
A Treasury of Nursery Rhymes originally published
in hardback in 1984
Reprinted 1987
Copyright © Kingfisher Books Limited 1984, 1986
All Rights Reserved

BRITISH LIBRARY CATALOGUING–IN–PUBLICATION DATA
Lullabies
   1. Lullabies, English – Texts
   I. Offen, Hilda
   784.6'2405   PR1195.L8
ISBN: 0 86272 226 8

Phototypeset by Tradespools Ltd, Frome,
Somerset
Printed in Spain.

HUSH-A-BYE

Hush-a-bye, baby, on the tree top,
When the wind blows, the cradle will rock;
When the bough breaks, the cradle will fall;
Down will come baby, cradle, and all.

PAT-A-CAKE, PAT-A-CAKE

Pat-a-cake, pat-a-cake, baker's man
Bake me a cake as fast as you can;
Pat it and prick it, and mark it with B
Put it in the oven for Baby and me.

PEASE PORRIDGE

Pease porridge hot,
Pease porridge cold,
Pease porridge in the pot,
Nine days old.
Some like it hot,
Some like it cold,
Some like it in the pot,
Nine days old.

HUSH-A-BYE

Hush-a-bye, baby, lie still with thy daddy,
Thy mammy has gone to the mill,
To get some meal to bake a cake,
So pray, my dear baby, lie still.

BABY BUNTING

Bye, baby bunting,
Daddy's gone a–hunting,
Gone to get a rabbit skin
To wrap the baby bunting in.

LITTLE BOY BLUE

Little Boy Blue,
    Come blow your horn.
The sheep's in the meadow,
    The cow's in the corn.

Where is the boy
    Who looks after the sheep?
He's under a haystack
    Fast asleep.

Will you wake him?
    No, not I,
For if I do,
    He's sure to cry.

BIRTHDAYS

Monday's child
is fair of face

Tuesday's child
is full of grace

Wednesday's child
is full of woe

Thursday's child
has far to go

Friday's child
is loving and giving

Saturday's child
works hard for its living

But the child that is born
on the Sabbath day
Is bonny and blithe,
and good and gay.

HUSH, LITTLE BABY

Hush, little baby, don't say a word,
Papa's going to buy you a mocking bird.

If the mocking bird won't sing,
Papa's going to buy you a diamond ring.

If the diamond ring turns to brass,
Papa's going to buy you a looking-glass.

If the looking-glass gets broke,
Papa's going to buy you a billy goat.

If that billy goat runs away,
Papa's going to buy you another today.

RIDE A COCK-HORSE

Ride a cock-horse to Banbury Cross,
To see a fine lady upon a white horse;
Rings on her fingers and bells on her toes,
She shall have music wherever she goes.

HUMPTY DUMPTY

Humpty Dumpty sat on a wall,
Humpty Dumpty had a great fall;
All the King's horses and all the King's men
Couldn't put Humpty together again.

WILLIE WINKIE

Wee Willie Winkie runs through the town,
Upstairs and downstairs in his nightgown,
Rapping at the window, crying through the lock,
Are all the children in their beds, it's past eight o'clock?

NIDDLEDY, NODDLEDY

Niddledy, noddledy
To and fro,
Tired and sleepy,
To bed we go,

Jump into bed,
Switch off the light,
Head on the pillow,
Shut your eyes tight.

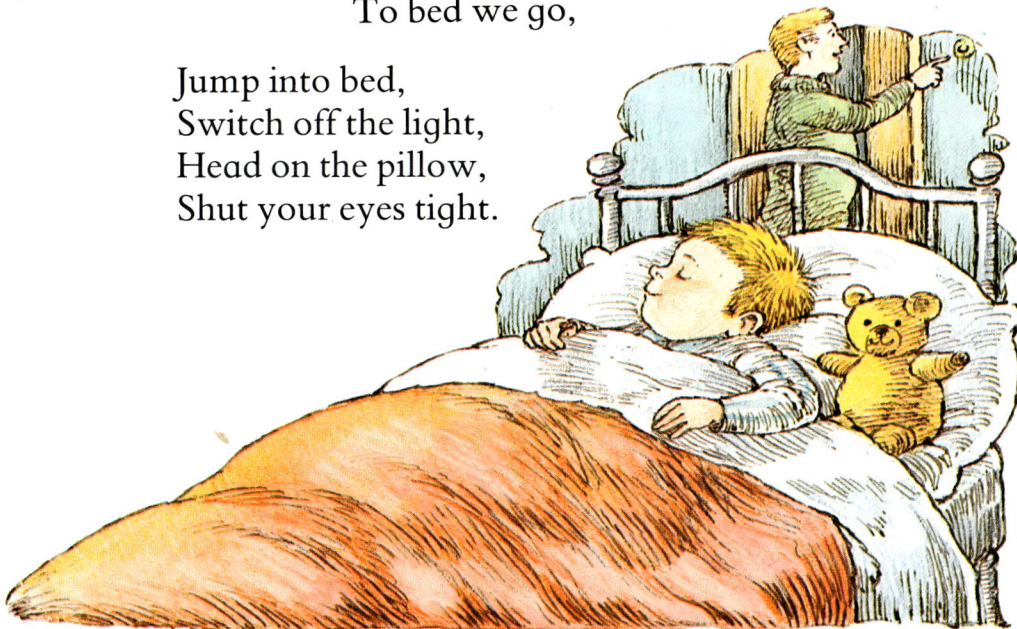

SLEEP, BABY, SLEEP

Sleep, baby, sleep,
   Our cottage vale is deep;
The little lamb is on the green
With woolly fleece so soft and clean –
   Sleep, baby, sleep.

Sleep, baby sleep,
   Down where the woodbines creep;
Be always like the lamb so mild,
A kind and sweet and gentle child,
   Sleep, baby, sleep.

THE LADYBIRD

Ladybird, ladybird,
   Fly away home,
Your house is on fire
   Your children all gone;
All but one,
   And her name is Ann,
And she has crept under
   The warming pan.

MY BLACK HEN

Hickety, pickety, my black hen,
She lays eggs for gentlemen;
Sometimes one, and sometimes ten,
Hickety, pickety, my black hen.

BAA, BAA, BLACK SHEEP

Baa, baa, black sheep,
 Have you any wool?
Yes, sir, yes, sir,
 Three bags full;
One for the master,
 And one for the dame,
And one for the little boy
 Who lives down the lane.

THIS LITTLE PIG WENT TO MARKET

This little pig went to market;
This little pig stayed at home;

This little pig had roast beef;
This little pig had none;
And this little pig cried, Wee-wee-wee,
And ran all the way home.

MOSES

Moses supposes his toeses are roses,
But Moses supposes erroneously;
For nobody's toeses are posies of roses
As Moses supposes his toeses to be.

ROCK-A-BABY

Rock-a-bye-baby,
    Thy cradle is green,
Father's a nobleman,
    Mother's a queen;
And Betty's a lady,
    And wears a gold ring;
And Johnny's a drummer,
    And drums for the king.

HUSH, MY BABY

Hush, my baby, do not cry,
Papa's coming by and by;
When he comes he'll come in a gig,
Hi cockalorum, jig, jig, jig.

THE CAT AND THE FIDDLE

Hey diddle, diddle, the cat and the fiddle,
The cow jumped over the moon;
The little dog laughed to see such sport,
And the dish ran away with the spoon.

LAVENDER'S BLUE

Lavender's blue, dilly, dilly,
  Lavender's green;
When I am King, dilly, dilly,
  You shall be Queen.

MARY, MARY

Mary, Mary, quite contrary,
  How does your garden grow?
With silver bells and cockle shells,
  And pretty maids all in a row.

ROSES ARE RED

Roses are red,
Violets are blue,
Sugar is sweet
And so are you.

BEDTIME

The Man in the Moon
Looked out of the moon,
Looked out of the moon and said,
"'Tis time for all children on the earth
To think about getting to bed!"

STAR LIGHT

Star light, star bright,
    First star I see tonight,
I wish I may, I wish I might
    Have the wish I wish tonight.

TWINKLE, TWINKLE

Twinkle, twinkle, little star,
How I wonder what you are!
Up above the world so high,
Like a diamond in the sky.

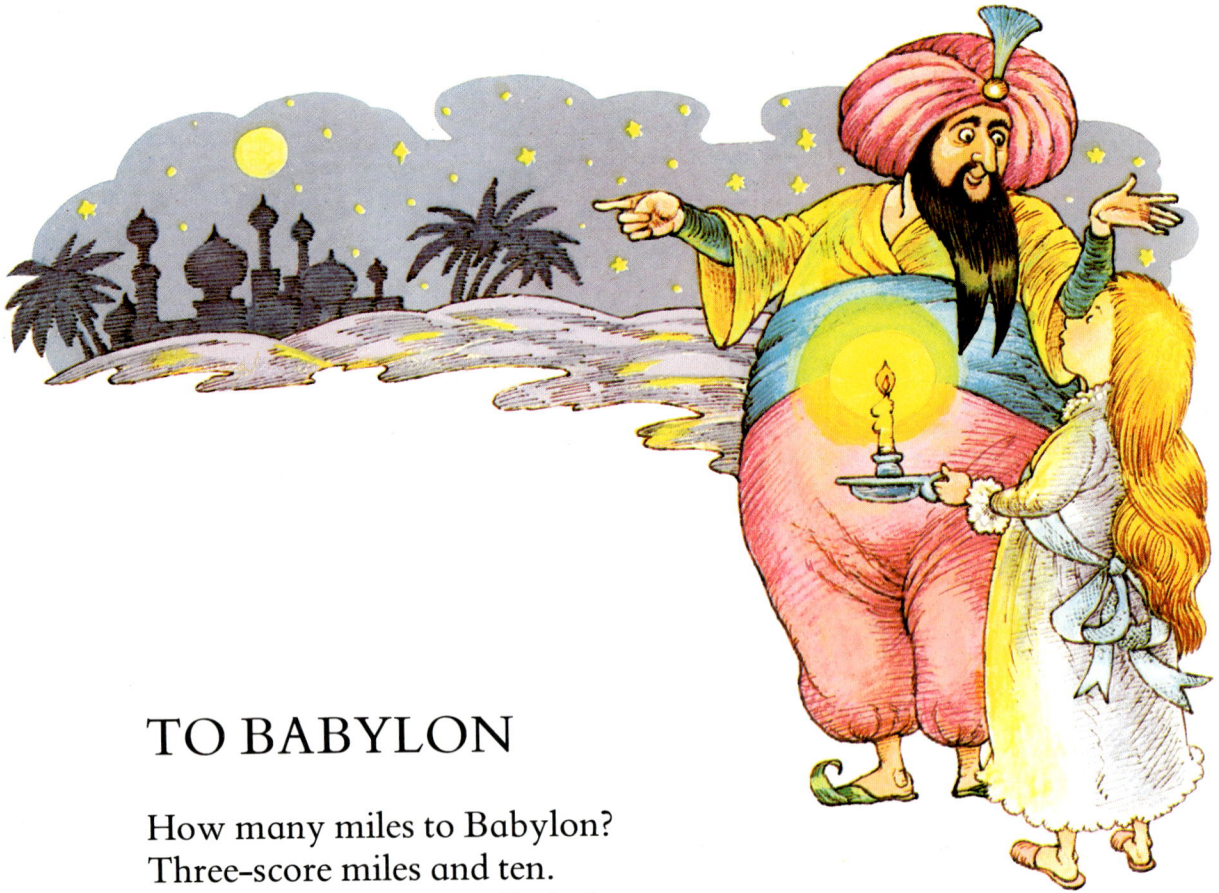

TO BABYLON

How many miles to Babylon?
Three-score miles and ten.
Can I get there by candle-light?
Yes, and back again.
If your heels are nimble and light,
You may get there by candle-light.

THE MOON

I see the moon,
And the moon sees me;
God bless the moon,
And God bless me.

BRING DADDY HOME

Bring Daddy home
  With a fiddle and a drum,
A pocket full of spices,
  An apple and a plum.

INDEX OF FIRST LINES